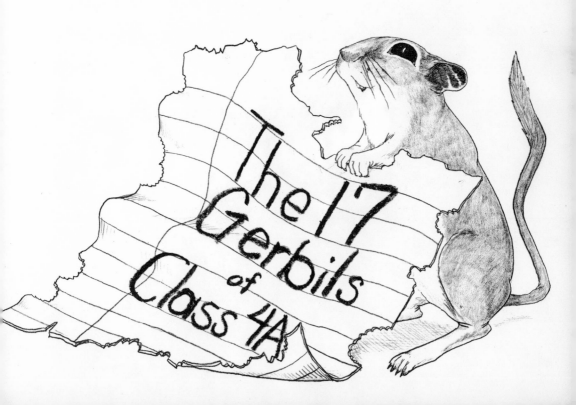

The 17 Gerbils of Class 4A

by William H. Hooks
pictures by Joel Schick

Coward, McCann + Geoghegan, Inc.
New York

The 17 Gerbils of Class 4A

Library of Congress Cataloging in Publication Data

Hooks, William A
The seventeen gerbils of class 4A.

SUMMARY: Three friends are faced with the dilemma
of how to dispose of the seventeen gerbils in
their classroom.
1. Gerbils—Legends and stories. [1. Gerbils
as pets—Fiction. 2. School stories] I. Title.
PZ10.3.H765Se [Fic] 75-28000
ISBN 0-698-20369-0
ISBN 0-698-30621-X lib. bdg.

PRINTED IN THE UNITED STATES OF AMERICA

To Nanny

1
Liberated Gerbils

"The end of the week they have to go. Now that's final. No discussion. No democratic procedure. Out! Just out!"

Josh hardly ever yelled at us like that. In fact, he was the one teacher who always let us talk things out. We even called him by his first name. "Make your own decisions. See if you can't figure it out for yourself," he was forever telling us.

So I guess he must have felt things were getting out of hand. Especially the animal life in our classroom. This time Josh was making the decisions all by himself. Well, if he hadn't yelled at us in such a loud voice, the gerbils wouldn't have started drumming their hind legs against their cages. They always do that when they get nervous.

Maybe I'd better tell you that we have seventeen gerbils in our room. And that makes thirty-four legs drumming away when they're nervous. That's just counting the back legs, of course.

From the sound of his voice, you could tell Josh meant to clean house. Schoolhouse, that is. Zero gerbils was his goal. And that meant a big problem for me and my friends, Cynthia and Tommy. The gerbils really belonged to the three of us. We sort of inherited them.

I signaled Cynthia and Tommy: Meet me at lunch.

Tommy gave me a V sign, which I took to mean "Okay." Cynthia winked her left eye— our secret signal for "Yes." She knew what our problem was.

I think I can honestly say that all twenty-two of us in 4A liked Josh. He was younger than most of our teachers. And he usually was pretty easygoing. But I think something snapped in him this morning.

Somebody left the cage door open. Just a tiny crack. But that's all an expert escape artist like a gerbil needs. Seven of our seventeen gerbils had liberated themselves. It took a half hour to round up all these fast-moving

liberated little pets. This wasn't the first time the gerbils had freed themselves, but never had so many escaped at once. Ordinarily, Cynthia or Tommy or I could handle a one-or-two-gerbil escape. But with seven of them scampering all over the room, Josh and the whole class joined in.

Who was to know that Mrs. Kraus, our principal, was going to pick this Monday morning to bring the new community school board members on a visit?

Her visit with us was a short one. Some of the kids never even knew we'd been visited. Mrs. Kraus mumbled something about a classroom experiment in animal recovery. Then she rushed the visitors out of our room. As he was leaving, one man exclaimed, "We put in a fat allowance for an exterminator. Why is this building overrun with mice?"

Josh crawled from under his desk just as Mrs. Kraus turned to look back into the room. Josh had this big pleased smile plastered across his face. He was holding a captured gerbil in one hand. His eyes met Mrs. Kraus' eyes. You've never seen a face change so quickly. He must have relaxed his grip on the gerbil, for the little animal escaped at just that moment. I wish Josh had stayed under the desk because, in my opinion, I don't think Mrs. Kraus believed Josh was *in* the room.

Well, Josh didn't yell at us at once. Not until we had unliberated the seven gerbils. As soon as they were back in their cages, he lowered the boom: "Friday they have to go!"

Exotic Pets

Before I go any further, I'd better tell you about Rogue. Because Rogue leads to gerbils, and gerbils leads to our problem. And it seemed that Josh meant business about solving that problem. By Friday afternoon!

Rogue was always bringing weirdo things to school. Things like Mexican jumping beans, bark fungus, hornets' nests, and snake skins. Josh was really super about all this stuff. And he helped us learn a lot about all those strange things. Josh said that Rogue's stuff made an exotic collection.

Cynthia called it "Rogue's *Yuck* Collection." And I pretty much agreed with her.

Rogue laughed and said, "Just call me Strange or *Mr. Exotic,* if you please."

So when Rogue turned up early one October morning with a surprise package, we all started guessing what it might be. Josh let us play around for a while. He usually gives us about ten minutes in the morning to settle down. There were some pretty wild guesses about what was in the box. But Rogue just smiled and said, "You're way off."

Finally, Cynthia said, "We're going at it all wrong. Give us a hint, Rogue. Is it animal, vegetable, or mineral?"

"Hint number one," boomed Rogue, sounding like the host on a TV quiz show. "Observe the holes punched in the sides of this recycled shoe box."

"It's animal!" shouted Cynthia.

"Guinea pig!"

"Rabbit?"

"Baby dragon."

"Kitten!"

"Is it a bird?"

Everyone was yelling and crowding around Rogue.

"Quiet or no see," shouted Rogue.

That shut up most of the class. Rogue made a big to-do waving his hands over the box and looking very mysterious. Then he lifted the lid, and there they were. Two little animals that looked like mice.

"Just a couple of old brown mice," said Tommy, sounding disappointed.

Everybody was sort of mumbling. You could feel the letdown all through the class. I don't know what we were expecting after Rogue's buildup, but he usually did better than mice. We'd had a family of white mice in the first grade.

"Take a closer look," said Rogue.

Cynthia pushed her way up to the box and said, "They've got fur on their tails. I never saw a mouse with fur on his tail before."

Then she started to pick up one of the little animals.

"Hold it," snapped Rogue. "You've got to be careful how you pick them up." Rogue reached in and picked one up. "You have to hold them real loose, with your hand gently cupped around them. Or you might scare them and get bitten.

"But you were on the right track, Cyn," Rogue continued. "They do have tails that are different from mice. See, the tail has fur all the way down, and there's a tuft of longer hairs at the end."

None of us had seen a mouse with a tail like that.

"Well, what are they?" asked Tommy.

"This," said Rogue in his best stage actor voice, "is a gerbil."

"A what?" two or three of us asked all at the same time.

"A gerbil. The nicest, cleanest pet you could ever own," announced Rogue.

Josh came over to see what was causing all the excitement. Before he could even get a peek into the box most of the class was yelling, "Josh, can we keep them?"

Josh looked kind of doubtful when he saw that it was two real live animals—not just a snake skin or a hornets' nest. But Josh says our classroom is really our own community, so he told us to make the decision. We let members of the class speak for and against keeping the gerbils. The "fors" made stronger speeches than the "againsts." But those who were not in favor of keeping the

gerbils brought up some interesting points to think about. Points like who was going to feed the gerbils, who was going to keep their house clean, and what was going to happen to the animals when the school term was over. These were good points, but most of the class was too excited about keeping the gerbils to pay much attention to them.

You can guess how the vote went. The gerbils were in to stay.

"Hey!" shouted Rogue. "I should properly introduce you to the newest members of our classroom community. Meet Maxi and Mini, our new exotic pets!"

3

Synonyms and Antonyms

"Friday they have to go!" I kept hearing Josh's words and wondering what we were going to do with seventeen gerbils. We'll just have to think of something at lunch today, I reassured myself. But I still couldn't keep my mind on synonyms and antonyms. That's what we were working on.

Yesterday antonyms had seemed interesting to me. And I loved the game Josh played with us where we had two teams. One team would yell out a word, and the other team had to come up with the opposite of it. That's antonyms for you.

My mind was on gerbils and I couldn't think of an antonym for "gerbil." But I could think of a good synonym. A word that meant

the same thing as "gerbil" had to be "trouble." That's what gerbils had become today—big trouble.

I gave up trying to follow the lesson. My mind kept going back to that October day when Rogue brought the first two gerbils to our class. It's hard to believe that it was only seven months ago.

We've had three generations of gerbils since then. Maxi and Mini have had babies twice. Talk about population explosion. These animals are only a little over a year old! Maybe Josh had some good reasons for going out of the gerbil business other than what happened when the principal brought the school board on a visit. It could be that he's getting worried about what could happen with seventeen gerbils in another year.

I'm not good at math in my head, but the possibilities seemed like an awful lot of gerbils.

My mind drifted back to Rogue and the first day he brought in the cute little rats. They're not really rats or even mice. Gerbils do belong to the rat family, but they are different. And they come from the far-off deserts of Asia. It's the Gobi Desert that's their real home.

But I'm getting off the track again. I've learned so much about gerbils this year I could probably pass a veterinary test.

Rogue caused a lot of excitement with Mini and Maxi that first day. Most of us kids had never seen a gerbil. None of us could tell which was Mini or which was Maxi.

"Mini's the girl, stupid," said Rogue.

Cynthia picked up both the gerbils and turned them upside down. Really gave them a scientific going-over. Josh says Cynthia has a lot of natural curiosity. She's nosy, all right, but she's my best friend.

"So what's different about Mini and Maxi?" asked Cynthia.

"Dum-dum, Maxi is a boy. Mini is a girl. And that's a difference," answered Rogue with his know-it-all smile.

"Come on, smart ass," says Tommy. "How *do* you tell the difference?" Tommy

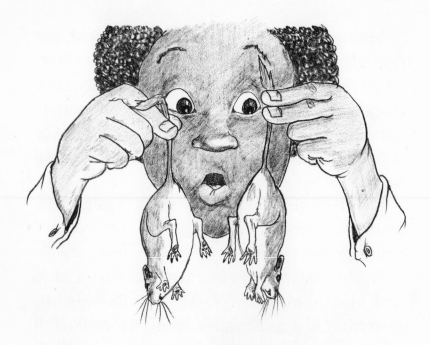

uses that term a lot. Especially if no teacher is listening. In the case of Rogue, I agree with Tommy. At least I halfway agree. I agree with the "smart" part. Rogue (although I've never admitted it to him) really is smart. In math he's practically a genius.

"Give up?" asked Rogue. "Okay. Maxi is the one with the little brown pouch under his belly, between his hind legs."

Rogue turned Maxi upside down, and sure enough there was a little brown pouch. Cynthia quickly flipped Mini over. No little brown pouch. Later on I found out you could also tell by the shape of their rear ends. Girl gerbils have a rounded bottom, and boy gerbils have a pointed backside.

Not to be outdone, Cynthia said, "A pink ribbon on Mini would be a lot easier way to tell who's who."

Josh had agreed we could keep the gerbils after Rogue, Cynthia, Tommy, and I promised to be responsible for them. Then he explained what he meant by responsible. If we took care of them. If we fed them, made them a house in the empty fish tank, and kept the house clean. *And* if all four of us made a science project out of Mini and Maxi.

I didn't know it that day, but I was on the way to become an expert on the rodent called *Gerbilus.* . . .

Suddenly I heard Josh call my name. He must have seen I was drifting away.

"Would you repeat the question again?" I asked, stalling for time.

"Give me a synonym for 'trouble,'" repeated Josh.

"Gerbils," I answered.

"Smart ass," whispered Tommy.

4
Footnotes

By the time we were finished with synonyms and antonyms it was still an hour till lunch. I thought the morning was never going to end. The gerbils had settled down to their favorite sport. Gnawing. All seventeen gerbils were busy gnawing away. All twenty-two of us were working on science projects.

When Rogue had first brought the gerbils to school, I thought something was wrong. Both Maxi and Mini spent 95 percent of their waking time gnawing. They chewed on everything in their cage. And if there was nothing in the cage to chew, they'd go to work on the cage itself. But we found out in our science study that Mini and Maxi were perfectly normal gerbils. They *have* to gnaw. Rogue said their motto was "Gnaw we must" because their front teeth never stop growing. And they have to keep them filed down. Can you imagine what would happen to a lazy gerbil?

Since we were now working in small groups on our science projects, I could get a word or two in to Tommy and Cynthia.

"What will your mother say when you come marching in with a happy, gnawing, leg-drumming, not to mention high-squeaking, well-adjusted gerbil family?" I whispered to Cynthia.

"I wouldn't put it to my mother in just that way," Cynthia hissed back to me.

"Well, how would you put it?" I breathed back at her.

"I'll have to think of something."

"You'd better think fast," I answered.

Tommy butted in and said he thought he could convince his father that gerbils were a good business. He figured he could go into business and sell them to pet shops. It looked like a quick way to make a fortune for him.

Josh drifted over in our direction, so I got busy with my science notebook. I was drawing pictures of the things gerbils like to play with most.

My number one thing was a cardboard tube. Gerbils are nuts about cardboard tubes. Or plastic tubes (but they're expensive). Or any other kind of tube. A gerbil would rather run through a tube than do anything else—except maybe gnaw.

Next to tubes, they like to climb little ladders. Sometimes they even line up to take turns going up and down the ladders. In third place I'd put mazes. They just love finding their way through mazes. And they're smart at it.

Gerbils need lots of exercise. It's pretty tough on them in a cage. So we got a little treadmill, and they kept it turning practically all the time. I made a really neat drawing of the treadmill in my notebook.

There's one thing that gerbils like to play with that you'd never guess. It's people. Gerbils like to explore people. Put some birdseed in your shirt pocket. Then place a gerbil on your shoulder (make sure it's a gerbil who knows you). Then watch him explore. It may tickle a little, but the gerbil will find his way into your pocket and sit there happily nibbling away.

I put a footnote at the bottom of my pictures of gerbil playthings. It says that the best way to catch a liberated gerbil is to put some bait, something like birdseed, in a cardboard tube. In goes the gerbil. He can't resist the double fun of birdseed and a tube. You pick up the tube. Quickly return gerbil to cage.

I think that footnote is going to make my science notebook look good. Maybe I'll think of some more footnotes.

Josh moved away from the gerbil cages where Tommy, Cynthia, and I were working. Two kids who were boiling some natural dyes were having what looked to me like a natural volcanic explosion. Josh headed to the rescue.

Now was my chance to get a few more words in to Tommy and Cynthia. "If Rogue were only here," I sighed.

"Yeah," said Tommy. "This is some problem he's left us."

Then Cynthia dropped her little bombshell. "Wait a minute," she said, with that natural curiosity look on her face. "From the looks of Mini, I'd say it won't be long before there'll be more gerbil proliferation!"

"Proliferation?" I looked closely at Mini and I could see what she meant, so I acted as if I'd been hearing that word all my life.

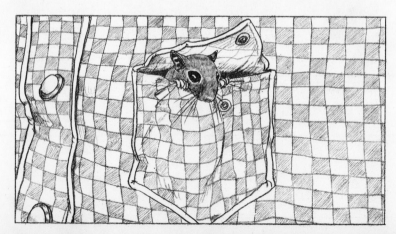

Proliferation

Josh had the natural dye business under control and was heading back in our direction. But he rushed right by us to help with a large, freshly painted, dripping mural which three kids were trying to hang in the art corner.

I started writing about how the gerbils liked to make tunnels in their cages. When we first made the cage, we put wood boards on the bottom. We added some paper towels and cedar shavings. In no time Maxi and Mini shredded up the towels and tried to dig into the shavings and shredded towels. Then they went to work on the wooden floor. They practically ate and scratched their way through it. Tommy asked, "Have we got beavers or gerbils here?"

Later we learned that gerbils dig fancy tunnels with connecting rooms when they are in the wild. To keep Maxi and Mini happy in their cage, we added a mound of dirt. They made the neatest tunnel and lost interest in trying to gnaw and dig through the floor.

Just as I finished writing about the tunnel, Tommy nudged me and whispered, "I'll bet Rogue would know what to do if he was here."

"Since Rogue is three thousand miles away, you'd better do some thinking yourself," snapped Cynthia.

And I was thinking about how Rogue came

to leave the gerbils to me and Cynthia and Tommy. . . .

At first Rogue did most of the chores for the gerbils, even though all four of us had promised to be responsible. You've got to remember—there was just Mini and Maxi. So Rogue didn't really need much help. But Tommy and Cynthia and I just sort of edged in.

Cynthia with her nosy—I mean inquiring— mind was a natural to help with the new pets. I didn't feel much one way or the other about that at first. But when your best friend spends most of her free time standing in front of a gerbil cage, you naturally wind up there, too.

Tommy was Rogue's buddy, so he was included in. Those were the good old days when we had the gerbils outnumbered four to two.

Well, a gerbil may be small. Mini was no more than four inches long, not counting the tail. But never underestimate the proliferation power of a gerbil.

To get quickly to the scientific facts, Mini had babies three weeks before Christmas vacation. Did she have babies! Wow! Seven of them!

When Tommy first saw the babies, he
yelled, "They're naked! What's wrong?"

Cynthia had read up on gerbils, so she
came back at him. "Mini's babies are perfectly normal. They are all born furless. And
if you'll take a good scientific look, you'll observe that their eyes aren't open yet."

Tommy muttered his usual.

Rogue laughed and said, "You won't know
these babies in a couple of weeks. They'll be
covered with fur, and their eyes will be open.
But what about some names? We need seven
new names!"

We were having a lot of fun with names for Mini's septuplets (that means seven babies). Finally Josh said why didn't we let the whole class in on the names. So we put every name on the board anyone wanted. Then everyone voted for just seven. We tallied up the vote and got the seven winning names:

1. Sheba
2. Clementine
3. Toyota
4. Satellite
5. Wiggler
6. Albert
7. Victoria

Now the numbers game was going the other way. Us caretakers—Tommy, Cynthia, Rogue, and me—were outnumbered four to nine. But the gerbils were still pretty easy to care for. On weekends we could leave enough food—things like birdseed, cabbage, carrots, celery, apples, and sunflower seeds. Gerbils don't need much water. Remember they come from the desert. If you leave things like lettuce and cabbage and celery, they can get plenty of water from the food. Gerbils also love fresh grass, dandelions, and clover. But you have to be sure that these things are not sprayed with insecticides.

And another important thing I almost forgot. You only have to clean the cage about every two weeks. So with four of us taking turns, cage changing only came up every other month.

Maxi helped Mini take care of the babies. He washed them and helped keep them rounded up. Baby gerbils are terribly active. Even before their eyes opened, they were wandering all over the cage. Maxi and Mini spent a lot of time trying to keep all seven babies in one spot. Mini nursed them for a little over three weeks. Then they started eating, and she weaned them. The babies liked uncooked oatmeal best.

Rogue said he thought we'd better build a new cage for Clementine, Toyota, Satellite, Sheba, Wiggler, Victoria, and Albert. I guess he had this proliferation problem in mind way back then.

So we put the gerbil children in a cage of their own. Cynthia brought up the "scientific" question: "Well, what about Mini and Maxi? Maybe it would be better to put all the ones with brown pouches in one cage and the gray bellies in another. This thing could get out of hand."

Rogue said that was a good idea. So we put the brown pouch ones in a cage with Maxi. And the gray bellies in the cage with Mini.

Some of the names didn't seem to fit when we made this separation. It turned out that Victoria had a brown pouch.

"Just call him Vic," Rogue said.

As I've told Cynthia many a time, the scientific method doesn't always work. Mini and Maxi missed each other so much, they wouldn't eat. The seven kid gerbils were great. But poor old Mini and Maxi just squeaked at each other and looked sad all the time.

For once I made a decision about the gerbils. We had to build another cage. Mini and Maxi were going to starve themselves to death if they couldn't stay together.

Back to the shop we went.

Our shop teacher, Mr. George, helped us with the new cage. Rogue and Cynthia drew the plans. They're better than Tommy and me with numbers and measuring. But I do remember that the cage was three feet long, eighteen inches wide, and eighteen inches high. We covered the sides and top with screen wire, but we built a good solid wooden floor. I should remember since Tommy and I were the ones who actually built the cage in shop. I guess you'd call Cynthia and Rogue the architects.

It was right after we built the new cage that Rogue left us. His family moved to California. I mean his regular family moved. But not his gerbil family. Rogue's parents said he could have Maxi and Mini sent out by plane later on. After they were settled in their new home.

Nothing much happened for a while after Rogue left.

Then one fine spring day Mini did it again! Only this time she had eight babies.

"Eight-tuplets!" I yelled when we got the final count.

"Octuplets, dum-dum," shouted Cynthia.

Then it hit me. We were running into a real number problem. The gerbils had jumped from nine to seventeen! Now that's proliferation for you. . . .

Tommy wrote to Rogue and told him about the new babies. Rogue wrote right back, *Airmail*. But the letter was very mysterious. There was a short note and a sealed envelope inside the letter. The note said Rogue and his family were living in an apartment temporarily, while they were looking for a house. He said he liked his school in San Jose and had a new friend named Miguel. The mysterious envelope was marked: TO BE OPENED ONLY IN CASE GERBILS ARE TO BE RELOCATED.

Josh's voice jerked my thoughts back to the present. To the new problem with the gerbils. The problem we had to settle by Friday.

A Will and a Problem

"Lunchtime in five minutes!" called Josh.

"Five minutes till lunchtime, and only four days till gerbil time," I muttered.

"Start putting your science projects to bed," Josh added.

Ha! Try putting a gerbil to bed in broad daylight when he's all excited. Since Cynthia and Tommy and I were eager to get to the lunchroom, we stashed our notebooks and got out our lunch boxes.

Cynthia called, "Hey, Tommy, bring that envelope Rogue sent us! I think we're going to need it." She always thinks ahead.

The three of us were the first ones to hit the cafeteria. So we didn't have long to stand in

line for the cold milk. The rest of our lunch
we bring from home. We picked a table way
in back and started.

Cynthia asked Tommy to open the envelope and read the paper. But Tommy was so
busy chewing he shoved it over to me.
"Yuread," he mumbled.

I ripped open the envelope and read
Rogue's message out loud.

Jan. 22nd

I, Rogue Johnson, hereby being of sound mind and body do will all my present and future gerbils to my three friends Tommy, Cynthia, and Chris.

The three before mentioned friends are to share the gerbils in the following way:

1) Tommy is to own 1/2 of them
2) Cynthia is to own 1/3 of them
3) Chris is to own 1/9 of them

Since it is hard to know how many gerbils you will have by the end of the school year, I think this will be the easy way to divide them up.

WITNESS TO THIS PAPER:

Miguel Ortiz

who I trust a lot.

SIGNED: _Rogue Johnson_

"Wow, that Rogue sounds like a real lawyer! He thinks of everything!" exclaimed Tommy.

I said, "That solves one part of our problem. Now we know how to divide the gerbils. I hope it will be as easy to convince our parents to let us bring them home."

"Rogue, what have you done to us?" moaned Cynthia.

All I could think of was how much I'd like to box up all these little pets and mail them to Rogue in California. The Johnson family had found a nice house in San Jose, California, but Rogue never sent for Maxi and Mini. He found out that there's a law in California that says NO GERBILS. California has a lot of desert, and they're afraid the gerbils will get loose and run wild. Proliferate all over the place and make big problems. So that's how I got the first thing anybody ever willed me.

Tommy stopped chewing long enough to say, "Okay, let's figure out how many gerbils each of us gets."

Cynthia whipped out her pencil (always prepared, that girl) and wrote down a big 17. Then this strange look came over her face.

"What's wrong, Cynthia?" I asked her.

"We're in big trouble again," she announced.

"What trouble?" piped Tommy. "I get half of them. That's simple enough."

"Tommy," asked Cynthia in her I'm-being-very-patient voice, "how can you take home half of seventeen gerbils?"

"In a box, stupid," Tommy said, getting kind of huffy.

"Dum-dum, think a sec," said Cynthia, still being *very* patient. "Seventeen. Seventeen! How can you take half of seventeen?"

"Oh," says Tommy. "That comes to eight and a half gerbils."

"Cynthia," I asked kind of quietly, "how are we going to get your third of seventeen?"

Well, Cynthia's quick. So she answered right back, "The same way we get your ninth of seventeen!"

A Dilemma

Cynthia very carefully put all the figures down on a piece of paper. First, she put a big 17 at the top of the page. Then she divided things up the way Rogue had left it in his will.

"Well, Tommy, you get half the gerbils. And that comes to exactly eight and one-half little animals, just as you figured," Cynthia announced.

"My third comes to five and two-thirds gerbils, and Chris, you get one and eight-ninths gerbils for your share." Cynthia held up the paper with her neat little rows of figures.

Tommy groaned, and I just sat still, trying to think of something clever to say.

Cynthia piped up, "Listen, fellows. We have a real dilemma!"

"We got enough trouble with the gerbils without bringing up something else," moaned Tommy.

I didn't know what a *dilemma* was, so I just kept quiet. I smiled at Cynthia and looked interested. I knew I could depend on Tommy to put his foot in.

"Tommy, a *dilemma* is when you have trouble and you don't know how to get out of it," Cynthia explained.

"Yes, Tommy, we have had a real gerbil dilemma since Josh made the announcement early this morning," I added. I told myself to hang on to that word. It could come in handy.

Cynthia was turning our dilemma around and around. "Now look at it this way," she said. "If it were apples or carrots instead of gerbils, you could just slice them up, and it would work out fine. But since it's gerbils, you run into the problem of who gets the front end and who gets the back end. That is, if you sliced them up."

"Stop, Cynthia!" I yelled at her. "No slicing up gerbils while we're eating lunch, please!"

Tommy didn't seem to mind the slicing up part since he kept right on eating. But something else was bothering him about Cynthia's plan.

"Slicing up gerbils might be a fair way to divide them." He paused to swallow. And I was thinking, even Tommy can't believe Cynthia was serious! Then he went on. "But it wouldn't do my plan to raise gerbils for sale any good. What could I do with a half a gerbil in a business like that?"

It's hard to know sometimes when Tommy is joking. Joking or not, I'd had enough.

"Shut up, both of you!" I shouted. "I've got a weak stomach! And it can't take sliced gerbils for lunch!"

I guess I was saved from losing two friends and my lunch by the bell. It screeched out the message that lunch was over, so we all headed back to our classroom.

Tommy was scratching his head and looking puzzled.

Cynthia had that faraway look she gets when she's turning a problem around scientifically.

I had a stomachache.

And all three of us were tromping back to class with a big fat dilemma on our hands.

A Solution

Before we got to the classroom, we could tell there was a lot of excitement. Kids were yelling and horsing around. My first thought was: *Gerbils! The gerbils are liberated again!*

Well, I was partly right. It was one gerbil out of his cage. Maxi. I could see someone holding Maxi. Rogue! It was Rogue. He was back to visit his grandmother. And his school and gerbil friends.

Tommy and Cynthia and I pushed our way over to Rogue, and everybody did a lot of friendly punching and horsing around. It got kind of crazy. Everybody talking and yelling at the same time. Poor old Maxi didn't understand what was going on. He let out a squeak and flew right out of Rogue's hand. Do I need to tell you that we almost replayed the same

scene that was going on when Mrs. Kraus, the principal, paid us her visit?

A frightened Maxi looked like at least seven liberated gerbils as he dashed from one spot to another. Tommy made a quick grab for Maxi and caught him by the tail.

What happened next scared the daylight out of me. Maxi pulled away, but the tuft of hair at the end of his tail was still in Tommy's hand.

"You've pulled his tail off!" screamed Cynthia.

"Oh, no, this couldn't happen to Maxi!" I groaned.

Tommy just stood there, staring at the tuft of hair in his hand.

"I didn't even pull very hard on his tail," explained Tommy. "Really I didn't."

For once Tommy looked like he was going to cry. I felt like I might be going to join him.

Rogue was doing the only sensible thing. He already had a cardboard tube ready to lure Maxi back into captivity.

Then Cynthia recovered and got a few sunflower seeds to put in the tube. Rogue pushed the tube to the edge of the bookcase under which Maxi was hiding.

Everybody quieted down. Without being told for a change. In a couple of seconds, Maxi had the scent of the sunflower seeds.

Very cautiously he crept into the tube. Then Rogue quickly got him back into the cage.

We all relaxed a little. All but poor Tommy, who was still holding the tuft of hair from Maxi's tail and looking very confused and guilty.

"Tommy, old buddy," said Rogue, "stop looking like you've ruined Maxi for life. It's perfectly normal for a gerbil to shed his tail tuft when under stress. That's a little trick nature has given him to help escape from traps and enemies. Sort of the way an iguana sheds his tail when you try to catch him. It doesn't hurt, and the spot heals over in a day or two."

"Will Maxi grow another tuft?" asked Tommy in a choked kind of voice.

"No," answered Rogue, "the spot will just heal, but no more hair will grow back. Look at it this way, Tommy. You'll never have any trouble telling which gerbil is Maxi. And believe me, Maxi is not vain about his looks. I doubt that he'll ever know the difference."

Josh came into the room, and he seemed pleased to have Rogue back for a visit. He asked Rogue to tell the class about his school in California.

Cynthia and Tommy and I thought we'd never get a chance to tell Rogue about our dilemma with the gerbils. But finally we did.

Rogue just smiled and said, "Don't worry, my good friends. I got you into this. Just watch me get you out. Right after school I'll solve the gerbil problem for you. Relax. No sweat, no problem. By the way, team, what names did you pick for Mini's last litter of babies?" Rogue asked.

"Do, Re, Mi, Fa, So, La, Ti, and Maxi Junior!" Tommy and Cynthia and I sang together.

Rogue really laughed at that. But he wouldn't tell us how he was going to solve our problem. I could hardly wait to find out what Rogue was going to do.

Finally, it was three o'clock and time for Rogue's magic act.

"Okay, Mr. Superfixer," said Cynthia. "Let's see you divide up these gerbils—without spilling any blood."

"Wait right here in front of the cages," Rogue said, acting very mysterious. "I'll be right back."

In a couple of minutes, he was back with another gerbil he had borrowed from the

room across the hall. Just what we needed! Rogue put a blue ribbon on this new gerbil. Then he put the borrowed gerbil in one of the cages.

"Now," said Rogue, "Tommy, how many gerbils do we have?"

"That makes eighteen now," answered Tommy. "But why?" Tommy asked, getting a little suspicious.

Rogue went on. "Tommy, choose half of the gerbils in the two cages. Go ahead, pick your half of the eighteen gerbils. But don't choose the one with the blue ribbon."

Tommy looked doubtful, but he went ahead and picked half of the eighteen. That came to nine whole gerbils. I noticed Tommy picked Mini first. Guess he thought she would be good for the business of raising gerbils.

Then Rogue said to Cynthia, "Okay, Cyn. Take a third of the eighteen gerbils. But skip the one with the blue ribbon."

"A third of eighteen is six," said Cynthia. "I know I can convince my mother to let me keep them." She sounded kind of uncertain for Cynthia. But she quickly picked out six of the gerbils.

"Now, Chris," said Rogue, "you take a ninth of the eighteen gerbils."

"A ninth of eighteen is two," I said out loud so they could all check me. So I took my two gerbils.

And you know what? There was still a gerbil left. The one with the blue ribbon was left over!

We couldn't believe it. We added it up again.

Tommy had nine.

Cynthia had six.

And I had two.

And nine and six and two make seventeen!

Rogue picked up the gerbil he had borrowed from across the hall and returned him. Then Rogue quickly said, "I've got to run, gang. How about you three coming over to Gram's house tonight?"

We agreed, though we felt a little dazed. It had been some day!

Our dilemma was solved. At least part of it was. We had the gerbils divided up. But none of us had counted on bringing gerbils home until school was out. We considered the gerbils ours, all right. In fact, we owned them legally. But neither Cynthia nor Tommy nor I had really settled it with our parents. We thought there was plenty of time to do that before summer vacation. Now all we had to do was convince our parents it was okay to take them home right away. That part seemed like it would be easy after what we had been through.

9
How Rogue Did It

By Friday Rogue had gone back to California, and our dilemma was about over.

My parents said it was okay for me to bring home my gerbils. They said they couldn't see any reason why I couldn't have two tiny little animals which I would be totally responsible for. I must honestly admit I didn't include the proliferation problem when I was convincing them it would be great to have gerbils.

Tommy had really sold his parents on his plan to raise gerbils for sale. He said his father was pleased as punch and thought Tommy was going to be a great entrepreneur. Tommy hasn't figured out what that means yet. But he says it must be good since his father is so pleased.

Cynthia's mother almost wrecked our plan. When she heard that Cyn was bringing home a half dozen animals she got worried. We didn't know for sure until Friday morning how Cynthia was going to make out. Knowing Cynthia, I shouldn't have worried. She finally convinced her mother that she could bring home all six of her gerbils . . . temporarily. Just until school was out. Then she would take four of the gerbils to her cousins for presents when she visited them in the summer.

Cynthia told me, "Chris, I can't make up my mind which four gerbils to give my cousins. It's tough—I want to keep them all. But a promise is a promise, and I'll just have to give them up. Too bad I had to tell my cousins about the surprise I'm bringing them." Ha, ha! They don't know what surprises they're going to get!

Everything was fine. Just fine. I don't think any of us realized how fond we were of these little animals. Taking care of them for almost a year had somehow made them a part of us. I guess we started off being curious and amused by them. But now I know how much I would miss the gentle tickle they make when they scrabble over my hands and arms.

The brightness of their berry-black eyes, the little pink sniffling noses, and the dandelion softness of their fur were things I had just been taking for granted. I thought, *Gee, it's wonderful that such small, delicate little animals could be such good friends with a giant like me*. I really loved them, and I could tell Cynthia did too.

I heard Tommy talking to Maxi when he thought no one was around. "Your tail is looking just fine, Maxi," he said. "And you know, Maxi, I may go into the gerbil business, but I'd never sell you or Mini." Then I knew Tommy felt the way Cynthia and I did about the gerbils.

Everything was fine—except Cynthia kept turning the old problem around in her head. She'd sigh every now and then and mutter, "How did Rogue do it?"

Finally she asked Josh for help. Josh did just what I expected—he turned our science project into a math project. He did give us one little hint. "Why don't you see if a half, a third, and a ninth add up to a hundred percent?"

Then he left us to make our own discovery.

Cynthia said, "Let's put it all in ninths." So we did.

A half would come to	4½ ninths
A third would come to	3 ninths
A ninth would come to	1 ninth
And that adds up to	8½ ninths

"That stinker!" yelled Cynthia. "I'll bet Rogue knew all the time that it wouldn't add up to a hundred percent."

"Yeah, that's right," agreed Tommy. "That's why he went and got another gerbil. That gerbil made it possible to divide them up!"

"You are brilliant, Tommy," said Cynthia.

"And that's why he had a gerbil left over when we all got our share," I chimed in.

"You, too, are brilliant," cried Cynthia.

We were all getting excited, and our voices were getting very loud. Josh rejoined us. I think he was listening all the time.

"I think you're all pretty brilliant!" Josh said.

Thirty-four gerbil legs began to drum against the floor of their cages.

I think they were applauding us.

More Facts from Chris' Science Notebook on Gerbils

First Gerbils in the United States

Gerbils first came to the United States in 1954. They were not considered pets at that time. Eight pairs of males and females, plus six extra males, were imported for scientific experiments. The thousands of gerbils that we have today all came from these twenty-two. In 1964, gerbils were first sold in pet stores.

* * * * * *

Gerbils and the Weather

Since gerbils come from the desert, you might think they would need a hot climate to do well. Not so. They can stand severe tem-

perature changes. That's because the deserts they come from are very hot during the day and very cold at night. You don't have to worry about gerbils getting too cold on weekends when the heat is very low in the school building. Gerbil pets would also do very well indoors even in a state like Alaska.

* * * * * *

A Scientific Observation

Gerbils always smell a new object in their cage before touching it.

* * * * * *

Hole Punchers

Gerbils are great hole punchers. Give a gerbil a sheet of paper, and he or she will bite neat little rows of holes all around the edges of the paper. They love doing this, and it's a fun way to have your gerbils perform for friends.

* * * * * *

Antelope Rats

Gerbils are sometimes called antelope rats. Their hind legs are longer and stronger than the front ones, and they can leap like an antelope.

* * * * * *

Claws and Ears

Strong claws and large ears help gerbils. With their claws they dig underground homes with connecting tunnels. They store their food underground and keep their babies there. Gerbils have big ears and very keen hearing. This helps them escape from enemies in the desert. I think it also may be why they get nervous when there is a lot of loud noise around them.

* * * * * *

Mazes

To make a good maze for gerbils to explore do the following:

1. Find several small cardboard boxes.
2. Cut off the tops.

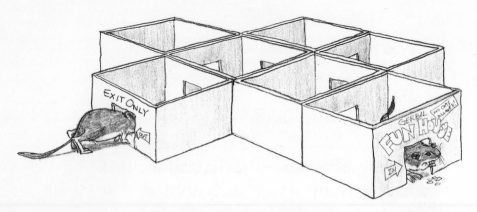

3. Glue the boxes together.
4. Cut small holes (just big enough for a gerbil to squeeze through) in the sides of the boxes so they all connect.
5. Make an entrance and an exit at opposite ends of the maze.

Gerbils will happily explore the maze many times. However, they will eventually chew it to pieces since it is cardboard. Then repeat steps 1 through 5 above.

* * * * * *

A Gerbil's Life Cycle

A gerbil is twenty-five days old when it is born. That is, it takes twenty-five days from the time the mother gerbil becomes pregnant until the babies are born.

Gerbils are about an inch long when they are born. Gerbils can have from one to ten babies at a time.

They are born naked but start growing a soft brown coat of fur by the time they are a week old.

Gerbils are also born with their eyes sealed. They open in about three weeks.

A mother gerbil weans her babies soon after their eyes open.

Within three months a gerbil is grown.

Gerbils live from three to five years.

When gerbils choose each other as mates, they choose for keeps. Even if one mate dies, the other may refuse to take another mate.

* * * * * *

A Conclusion

It's easy to get hooked on gerbils.